By the same author

Going Shopping　　Going Swimming
Doing The Washing　Going To Playschool
Having A Picnic　　Doing The Garden
Coming To Tea　　Polly's Puffin
Tex The Cowboy

For Tim and the children at Spinney Hill School

5 7 9 10 8 6 4

Copyright © Sarah Garland 1994

The right of Sarah Garland to be identified
as the author and illustrator of this work
has been asserted under the Copyright,
Designs and Patents Act, 1988

First published in Great Britain 1994 by
The Bodley Head Children's Books
An imprint of Random House UK Ltd
20 Vauxhall Bridge Road
London SW1V 2SA

Designed by Rowan Seymour
Printed and bound in China

A catalogue record for this book is available from the
British Library

ISBN 0 370 31858 7

PASS IT, POLLY

Sarah Garland

The Bodley Head
London

Polly's school is Belmont Primary.
Polly's teacher is Mr Budd.

On Monday Mr Budd said:

Polly and Nisha were the only girls who put their hands up.

After lunch they got ready for their first practice game.

But, the practice game did not go well.

It went very badly.

Polly and Nisha were muddy and cross.

They decided to look for a football book in the library.

They learnt some interesting things about fairies, fishes, fossils and Finland, but nothing very helpful about football.

They had tea at Polly's house.

But the next day was not much better

and they went back to Nisha's house after school feeling quite fed up.

Grandpa could remember and, after tea, he began to teach them all he knew.

On Tuesday he taught them how to pass the ball and how to stop it.

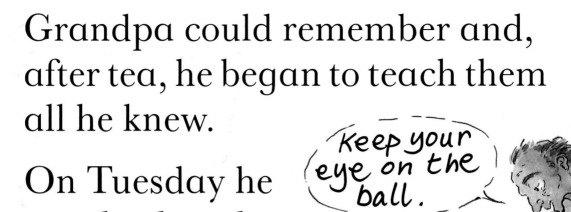

On Wednesday he taught them how to head the ball and how to dribble.

On Thursday he taught them how to trap the ball and how to throw it in.

And on Friday he taught them how to score a goal.

On Saturday the coach from
Greenhill School arrived.

pheeeeeeeeee

Kick off!
The match began!
Nisha dribbled up the field and
passed to Kiran.

Kiran passed to Polly.

Polly headed to Pete.

Pete put it in the net!

The game was fast and furious!
Belmont School had one goal, but
soon Greenhill School had two!

But a big boy from Greenhill was out to get Polly.

He raced up behind her and stuck out his foot – a dirty trick!

Polly jumped!   She swerved!

She kicked the ball right between the posts!

GOAL!

Just as the final whistle blew.

- Pheeeeeeeee

The match was a draw!

Mr Budd asked Mr Patel to help coach the football team.